Joan Aiken was born in Sussex, not far from where she lives now, and grew up with her mother and stepfather, the English writer Martin Armstrong. Her father was the American poet, Conrad Aiken. She began writing at the age of five, and hasn't stopped since; alongside two marriages and two children. Since the early 1960s, over ninety of her books have been published for both children and adults. Joan Aiken's spellbinding power to captivate readers both young and old grows with every story written.

The Jewel Seed

Joan Aiken

Illustrated by Peter Bailey

Hodder
Children's
Books

a division of Hodder Headline plc

A Catalogue record for this book is available from the British Library

ISBN 0 340 68133 0

Printed and bound in Great Britain by
Mackays of Chatham plc, Chatham, Kent

Hodder Children's Books
A Division of Hodder Headline plc
338 Euston Road
London NW1 3BH

In memory of my father,
the poet Conrad Aiken, who told a story,
"The Jewel Seed", when I was too young to
remember.

Chapter One

The graduation ceremony of the Grand and Ancient College of Siberian Witches is an impressive affair. It takes place far to the north, on the Taymir Peninsula, in winter darkness, and inside the draughty structure of what used to be a huge aircraft hangar. Long since abandoned by the military, it now easily accommodates the nine thousand nine hundred and ninety-nine delegates and candidates who make their way to the conference from all parts of the world.

The proceedings of the meeting are transacted in low whispers, which makes them all the more solemn and mysterious; the only loud sounds to be heard are the crackle of ice and the howling of the north wind overhead; the only light comes from the red-and-green streamers of the aurora borealis in the sky, observable now and then through gaps in the disintegrating roof.

At the finish of last year's ceremony the chairperson of the conference suddenly departed from the normal procedure by tapping three times with an icicle on the speaker's rostrum, and then surprised the delegates by ordering them to wait a moment before taking their leave.

"Sisters – brethren – one final word!"

The masked, mortarboarded, black-garbed assembly waited, standing in motionless suspense. The northerly gale shrieked overhead.

"A warning! An injunction! A message! Word has just come to us that the Wanderer is abroad. I will not mention any of his forty-nine names. You all know to whom I refer."

An assenting shiver ran through the multitude.

"He is abroad in quest of the lost Jewel Seed."

Another quiver among the black-robed listeners.

9

"The Jewel Seed, as you well know, is a compressed universe. It was lost, aeons ago, in a handful of flax seed given to a shepherd by Holda, the goddess, one of our most powerful enemies. One that we would dearly like to see shackled in dark for evermore. The finder of that seed, by means of the necessary password, can unlock it and release from it all knowledge, all science, history, art, magic, craft - *power*. If we, the Winter People, can find this tiny treasure, total dominion over all space will be ours; another, and far more terrible Winter War can be set in motion. Chaos will come again."

A ripple of high satisfaction at this prospect ran through the dark congregation.

"But," whispered nine thousand nine hundred and ninety-nine voices, "*where* is it? Where is the Jewel Seed to be found? Where is it hidden?"

"That, we are not certain. Long ago, Holda, the goddess, gave a handful of flax

10

seeds to a shepherd. The Jewel Seed had fallen from her necklace into the handful of tiny grains. Since then it has never been seen . . . It was thought to have lodged inside a Black Hole. But, if the Wanderer is abroad, this must mean that he has news of it. Be alert, sisters and brothers! At the first hint of its whereabouts, call me! Call me! And I shall come speeding . . ."

With that, the multitude dispersed, some of them embarking on their ships made from fingernails, others riding on broomsticks, others transforming themselves into reindeer, elk, or migratory birds.

And one, on a bicycle made of fingernails, took her way towards England, to the County of Hussex, to Sesame Green. She knew more about the Jewel Seed than the rest of her colleagues. But she intended to keep the knowledge to herself.

Chapter Two

When Nonnie Smith left her granny's house at Sesame Green and went to live with her London cousins, the Sculpins, wearing a stolen shirt, various unexpected things began to happen.

For a start, Nonnie didn't know the shirt was stolen. (It had in fact been stolen not once, but twice.)

Nonnie's school-leaving report said that she was a kind, friendly girl, not the world's wonder at passing exams, but clever with her hands, and a fine flute-player.

She had recently had a letter from her elder sister, Una, promising to find her a job as a trainee-hairdresser at Kirlylox Ltd., Forge Hill, London, where Una had worked for the last five years.

"Yes, it's certainly best you should go to London, dearie," Granny Smith told Nonnie. "You can lodge with your Aunt Daisy at first, in Rumbury Town; and you'll maybe get a chance to play with one of those music-groups in your free time. For there beant no kind of living round Sesame Green from playing the flute - not for a gal your age. No, you'll do better in the city. So you just pack up your things and catch the eight-thirty bus from Fourways Corner tomorrow morning."

Nonnie sighed. She hated to leave her grandmother, but she could see plainly that the old lady was tired and wanted some peace and privacy.

Granny Smith had brought up Nonnie, and her eight elder brothers and sisters, since the day that their parents, who were climbers, fell off the side of a mountain in Tibet. Una, the eldest, had become a hairdresser, Duessa, the next, went into dentistry, Teresa got a job in television,

Quad, a tough boy, learned blacksmithing, Quintus, who never grew very tall and liked horses, became a jockey, Sextus turned to baking, Seppy took to carpentry, and Octavia worked in a newspaper office.

Nonnie was the last to leave and, though Granny Smith had been very fond of them all, anyone could see that she really looked forward to no more heaps of clothes all over the floor, no more midnight snacks, no more non-stop TV.

In fact, Granny Smith had her future firmly planned out.

"But first we must find you a white shirt," she told Nonnie. "For a job interview you definitely need a white shirt and a black skirt."

Nonnie didn't really see the necessity for this. She suspected that hairdressers might have changed their ways since Granny Smith last went to London in Festival-of-Britain year. But she was busy clearing out the bedroom she had shared with Tess and Tavey, packing up her flute, her music, three pairs of jeans, six T-shirts, and her collection of five tiny enamel snuff-boxes; she didn't pay a lot of attention to what her grandmother was saying.

Meanwhile Granny Smith walked quietly into the terribly tangled and untidy garden of their neighbour, Mrs Wednesday, and removed a white shirt which had been hanging on the clothesline there for the past five weeks.

"I reckon Mrs Wednesday won't ever be coming back from her trip. Something unexpected or nasty must have happened to her at that Siberian conference. Or – if she *does* come back – she can hardly expect to find the shirt still hanging on the line after all this time. A gale might have blown it away. There's been lots of autumn gales lately."

Thus reasoned Granny Smith to herself, and she took down the shirt, which was, indeed, bleached remarkably white by all the rain that had fallen in the last five weeks since Mrs Wednesday had left to attend a conference in Siberia, on the Taymir Peninsula. "Which, from there," she had told Granny Smith, "you can't get much farther north without bumping into the North Pole. And it's so quiet that people go there just to listen to the silence. If ever the wind stops blowing."

"Maybe Mrs W *did* bump into the North Pole," thought Granny Smith, as she took down the snowy-white shirt. "In which case there's no need for argufication. Anyhow, Nonnie can always buy her another shirt out of her first week's pay packet. Least said, soonest mended, is what *I* always say."

So all she said to Nonnie, handing her the shirt, was, "Just fancy! Well I never! This shirt's got your sister Una's initials embroidered; must be the one she made herself at school. I always did think that Mrs Wednesday was a bit light-fingered,

now I'm sure of it. If she doesn't ever come back it'll be no loss to the neighbourhood. Now don't you cry, Nonnie dear; just put on the shirt and off you go."

"Yes, Grandma," said Nonnie. She put on the shirt (it was rather too big and the sleeves were much too long) over a black skirt remaining from school uniform. Then, her eyes streaming with tears, she hugged her granny a great many times, shouldered her backpack, and climbed on board the eight-thirty bus from Fourways Corner to Euston Station, London.

"And that's the last of them settled in life," thought Granny Smith, heaving a huge breath of satisfaction. And she stopped at the public callbox by the pub to phone Mr Tidy, the undertaker, and ask him to come and pick her up tomorrow. She walked home, ate a delicious bowl of soup, went to bed, and died peacefully in her sleep at the age of ninety-eight. "Who wants to live to a hundred?" was her last thought.

Meanwhile, unaware of this, Nonnie travelled up to London and made her way to the house of her aunt Daisy Sculpin at Number Five, Pond Walk, Rumbury Town.

Not long after, Granny Smith's neighbour, Mrs Wednesday, (who, travelling back from the Taymir Peninsula to Sesame Green on her bike made of fingernails, had been delayed on the last stage of her journey by several punctures) finally arrived at her cottage and was greatly startled and annoyed to find that, during her absence from home, her long-time neighbour Mrs Smith had died, the last grandchild, Nonnie, had left home, and the next-door house was now occupied by a young couple, the Griddles, with their baby and eleven poodles. The atmosphere was not restful. And: "*Where* is my white shirt that I left hanging on the line?" demanded Mrs Wednesday of her new neighbours. "That shirt was supposed to hang on that line for forty-nine days."

But the Griddles knew nothing of any shirt. Nor could they tell Mrs Wednesday where Nonnie had gone.

"Maybe to one of her brothers or sisters ... somewhere in London, I expect ..." Mrs Griddle said vaguely.

However at the village Post Office they were able to inform Mrs Wednesday that the eldest grandchild, Una Smith, had a job at Kirlylox hairdressers in Forge Hill. "We saw her two weeks ago in the street at

Forge Hill being interviewed by that television fellow, Lucky Lukie. She was outside the shop."

"Oh, pounce and powderation," said Mrs Wednesday to herself very sourly. "This calls for retro-active sorcery, which is always plaguey hard work."

And she began collecting fingernails and snippets of human hair in order to build a needfire, and so work her way backwards in time.

Chapter Three

$\mathcal{M}$rs Daisy Sculpin lived with her son John in Rumbury Town, which is an ancient, dusty, twisty, cobbly, narrow-laned quarter of north London. It has a canal, a hill, several venerable rail stations, an overgrown cemetery, a stretch of marshland known as Rumbury Waste, rows of little shops selling very odd goods, and some extremely ancient houses. That of John and his mother carried a round blue sign like a plate over the front door which said: Marcus Magus, Alchymyste, dwelte in Ysse Howse inne Fyfteene Syxtye.

The house was very cornery and cupboardy. It had a strong, agreeable smell of tar and spices. "That's because it was built from ships' timbers," John Sculpin told his cousin, taking her up to a tiny room on the top floor. She had been to the house before, but not since she was much smaller, and never upstairs.

"Is the house haunted?" asked Nonnie hopefully, admiring her attic, which had a ceiling that sloped right down to the floor, and two dormer windows.

"Only sometimes," said John. "Ma said she was sorry to put you in the attic—"

"I love it," said Nonnie, looking out over the rainy roofs of Rumbury Town, and the green expanse of Rumbury Waste, to the Post Office Tower, which rose like a spider's leg in the distance.

"—But she has just let the best guest room to a lodger for a month. He's doing research at the Unwellcome Institute, and he pays rent, and has his cat along with him, and pays rent for the cat as well, so he needs a big room."

"What's his name?"

"Colonel Njm.   He comes from

Ljpljnd. And his cat's called Hrjgff. It stays shut up in his room, which is just as well, for Euston can't stand it."

"Who's Euston?"

"Our cat," said John, leading the way downstairs again. "That's him now, telling Hrjgff where he gets off."

Euston was outside the closed guest room door. He was a large, muscular cat, pale putty-colour with a touch of powdered ginger, white whiskers, and gold eyes. He was in a bristling rage, growling under his breath in one long, continuous diatribe of bad language. A ferocious hissing responded from inside the visitor's door.

"Come on downstairs, Euston, that's not polite to lodgers." John picked up the cat and carried him, sulking, down to the kitchen, where Mrs Sculpin, Aunt Daisy, was preparing an early festive tea of hot buttered cinnamon toast, pancakes, and sardine sandwiches. Some of the sardine sandwiches placated Euston – a little.

Mrs Sculpin, Aunt Daisy, was a thin, refined-looking lady. Her expression was wistful, as if she had resigned herself to not getting much fun out of life. Actually she got a good deal of fun, for she enjoyed going to auction sales, where she bought all kinds of interesting articles, very cheap. Today she had bought a cuckoo clock which would also make toast, a set of sensor lights, a microwave oven, and a spinning-wheel. Most of these articles needed repair, but John was quite handy at that.

Also, Mrs Sculpin enjoyed letting her guest room to lodgers, who came and went so often that there was no time for them to become boring or disagreeable.

"My sister Una used to spin," said Nonnie, looking at the broken spinning-wheel with interest. "I'd like to have a try at that."

"One of these Sundays," said John, "when I've mended it, we'll go down to the llama house at the zoo and pick some wool off the railings."

While they were still eating tea they heard the front door bang.

"That'll be the Colonel," said Mrs Sculpin, and she called, "Oh, Colonel, would you like a nice cup of tea?"

Colonel Njm put his head round the kitchen door, bringing an icy draught with him. He was a tall, massive man, with a white beard. He wore a dark grey suit, a long dark duffel coat, and a hat with a very broad brim, pulled right down over one side of his face.

"I thank you, Mrs Sculpin, no; I partook of refreshment at the Institute."

"Here's my niece Nonnie, who's just come to stop with us," said Mrs Sculpin.

Nonnie, who had just taken a large mouthful of cinnamon toast, swallowed it down and nodded politely. Colonel Njm fixed her with such a severe and glittering eye that she felt as if she had been obliged to fill in some huge form about herself, and had made a shocking mess of it. But the Colonel said nothing, only inclined his head courteously and turned to go upstairs.

"I'll bring you up a bit of dinner presently, Colonel, if you aren't going out," Mrs Sculpin called after him.

"Very kind . . ." his deep voice floated back.

"He works away at his computer up there," Mrs Sculpin told Nonnie. "Don't *ever* let his cat out, no matter how much it hisses, Nonnie, for I hate to think what it and Euston might do to each other. Mincemeat! John, if you've finished your tea, do you want to fix up those sensor lights in the back yard? There's been ever such a lot of burglaries lately in Rumbury Town, let alone houses being set fire to, and the police can't seem to lay hands on the malefactors; I can't think what gets into people. Now, after tea, Nonnie, I expect you'll want to go and see your sister Una. Do you remember the way? You went to see her the last time you came and stayed with us, didn't you? She said she'd be expecting you. It's a nuisance us having no phone in the house, we've tried various times, but all we get is the voice of the ghost, so we've given up."

"What does he say?" asked Nonnie.

"Sometimes he says 'Beware' (but we don't know what of, he doesn't tell us, so that's not much help). Sometimes he says 'Time is elastic', or 'Wisdom is its own reward'. We don't take much notice. But anyway your sis is expecting you. I went up to Kirlylox last week and had a nice perm."

Aunt Daisy's hair was set in rather spidery grey curls all over her head.

"I asked Una if she'd like to come and live here when Colonel Njm goes, but she said 'no, thank you,' she's sharing a flat with two girls. But she sent her best love and says she's longing to see you, ducks."

"And I'm longing to see her," said Nonnie.

Though the eldest, separated from her by nine years, Una had always been Nonnie's special sister, never too busy to listen, or too bossy to help, always ready with advice over homework or a wonderful story to tell. There was something about Una's stories, Nonnie thought, that was almost magic; they were quite unlike any other stories; they took you away to a wonderful land, full of glittering immortal beings and mysteries. And she was beautiful, with long shining hair the colour of raw silk.

So, after tea, John showed his cousin the way to Rumbury Tube Station, and told her which train to take for Forge Hill.

"It's the Mewing Line. I'd come too, but I've a job to do right here, in the station."

John's job was erasing Objectionable Inscriptions chalked or painted on walls in London tube stations. He worked long hours at this, and travelled all over London on his bike, carrying a bucket and mop and flask of eraser fluid.

"Wouldn't it be quicker to go by tube?" Nonnie asked, but he shook his head. "Bike's much faster. Now, you go five stops, northbound, to Forge Hill, and the Kirlylox shop is just across the road from the tube station, on the right in the shopping arcade."

He started scrubbing at some large red-painted words which said: BEWAIR OV THE BOTLAICE MONSTAR.

"What's the Bootlace Monster?" asked Nonnie, watching him work as she waited for her northbound train.

"Oh yes! Mum said, be sure to warn you," John told her. "*Never* walk along the canal towpath after dark. There's a monster in the canal – or so people say – it swallows you, all but your bootlaces. It spits them out."

"Suppose you don't wear boots with laces?"

John scratched his head.

"Maybe it would spit out your bus pass or false teeth instead. Some people think it's the Loch Ness Monster come south along the waterways from Scotland."

A northbound train pulled into the station, the doors opened, and Nonnie stepped aboard.

"See you at suppertime!" called John as the door closed. Then, having erased the inscription, he went home to work on the sensor lights in the back yard. Euston the cat sat watching him from the top of the rain water barrel.

"And *you'd* better stop indoors at night, Euston, or you'll be setting them off all the time," John told him. Euston blinked haughtily, then stared up in a meaningful manner at Colonel Njm's window, which was set just above the gable of the bathroom roof.

"You mean Colonel Njm's cat comes out that way? All the more reason for you to stay in at night," said John.

Strangely enough, when Nonnie got out of the train at Forge Hill, and crossed the street to the shopping mall, she could find no hairdressing establishment called Kirlylox. The first shop on the right was an open-fronted clothes market with clumps and racks of brilliantly coloured shirts and pants and tunics and skirts hanging on metal rails, red and pink lights glowing overhead, and a roar of rock music. A small black stuffed witch dangled above the clothes holding a sign which said: SHOPLIFTERS WILL BE CURSED.

The name of the shop was Mrs Wednesday's.

Chapter Four

"Well I never! What do you know about that?" exclaimed Mrs Sculpin sympathetically, when Nonnie returned to Number Five, Pond Walk. "Kirlylox all closed down? And no sign of your sister Una? It's a proper shame the way shops suddenly go bankrupt and shut down without a word of warning; you can't depend on the same place from one week to the next. But still, you can be sure that Una will get in touch with you very soon, dearie; she's probably busy finding herself another job."

"You don't have the address of her flat?"

"No, lovey. What you'd best do is go back to that shop – Wednesday's, did you say it was called? – and ask the girls there if they know where the Kirlylox lot went."

"Yes. I should have thought of that. It was such a nasty place, though," Nonnie said, frowning thoughtfully.

"Nasty, love? How can a clothes shop be *nasty*?" Mrs Sculpin was surprised.

"Oh – I don't know. The colours of the clothes were ugly. The lights were much too bright – blinding – and the music was too loud. And I didn't like the way the salesgirls looked at me – as if the clothes I had on were dowdy and old-fashioned. One of them called out in a kind of a jeering voice, 'Want a new shirt, Soapy?'"

"Oh, it's no use taking notice of such talk," said Mrs Sculpin. "But still, if I was you, I'd keep that black skirt and that shirt for best – white picks up the dirt shockingly in London. If you like, you can put the shirt in now, with the Colonel's wash and hang it out in the back yard. I do the Colonel's smalls for him every day; *very* particular, he is; and very thick his under-things are, made of goats' hair or something like; it's lucky I've the washing machine I picked up for five pounds in Rumbury Market."

So Nonnie unpacked her bag and changed into a T-shirt and jeans. Wrapped in the jeans was a present she had brought for her sister. When their parents were still alive, in Tibet, they had posted home a bundle of gifts for all their children. The parcel had taken years to arrive and had not been received until after the senders were dead. There had been a pair of unusual Tibetan scissors for Una, made of copper, an ivory toothpick for Duessa, a pen for Octavia, a copper hammer for Quad, a little bone pipe for Nonnie . . . all the others had received their gifts but Una was away from home when the package arrived, so Nonnie had brought the scissors to London, and now slipped them into her jeans pocket, in case Una turned up.

After Nonnie had washed her shirt and hung it out – there was a good deal of noise, was it birds flapping in the elder tree at the end of the yard? – Aunt Daisy said, "Dearie, would you like to step up the stairs with the Colonel's meal while I dish up for the rest of us?"

"Yes, of course, Aunt Daisy."

Nonnie took the tray, which held a plateful of smoking-hot beef pie and vegetables, a mug of beer, brown bread roll, and a dish of rice pudding with raisins. She knocked at the guest room door and heard a loud hiss from inside. Then there was a kind of scuffle. After a considerable pause, a voice called, "Come in."

Entering, Nonnie looked around her for the Colonel's cat. But, strangely enough, it was not to be seen. She did notice, though, on the bedside table, a tray full of sand – for the cat? – and, on the mantelpiece, two huge black birds, motion-less, apparently stuffed. But most of her attention was taken by a big, beautiful globe on a stand. It was rather larger than a TV set and had a relief map of the world on its surface with what looked like real grass and tiny trees growing, and rocky mountains. A red light glowed at the point where London would be in the British Isles.

"Thank you, child," said Colonel Njm, receiving the supper tray, and he placed it on a table which stood in the bay window. Doing so, he passed near the sand tray and as he went by the sand swished about and formed itself into a series of lines and hooks and swags and circles. On the table stood a computer console and screen. The screen came to life and displayed the same symbols as the sand on the tray. Colonel Njm waved an impatient hand at both. Quickly, the screen went blank and the sand smoothed itself out.

"I'll come back for the tray later, shall I?" Nonnie offered. "Doesn't your cat want any dinner? Euston likes coley-fish."

"Thank you, no, child," replied the Colonel absently, seating himself. "My pet looks after his own requirements."

Oh well, Nonnie thought, running downstairs, I suppose there must be lots of mice in a house as old as this.

"Does the Colonel always wear his hat in the house?" she asked her aunt.

"Yes, always. Perhaps because he has only one eye, poor man."

"*Has* he? I didn't notice that."

John came in from working on the yard lights and was helped to pie. He was surprised and sorry to hear that his cousin Una and the Kirlylox shop had gone from Forge Hill High Street.

"How about advertising for Una in the Rumbury Gazette?" he suggested.

"Not a bad idea, if she doesn't get in touch soon."

After they had washed the dishes, Nonnie went out to the brick-paved back yard to fetch in the washing. It was a dank, cold, foggy evening. John's sensor lights flashed on brilliantly as she walked to the clothesline. She found that Colonel Njm's long, heavy underwear had frozen as stiff as oak planking. Whereas Una's white shirt was quite soft and dry and felt warm.

"Just hang the Colonel's things on the airer in the scullery, love," said Mrs Sculpin. "They'll dry overnight."

"I believe there was some creature scuffling about at the far end of the yard, Aunt Daisy. Something seemed to be flapping and panting in that big elder tree," said Nonnie, very glad to be back in the light and warmth of the kitchen. "John's lights don't reach as far as that."

"Maybe it was the Colonel's cat, I think it goes out over the roof," said her aunt. "Now - won't you and John give us a little music, dearie?"

John, it turned out, was a skilful performer on the triangle, and played in the Rumbury Town Percussion Band. So, for an hour, he and Nonnie entertained Mrs Sculpin with beautiful flute-and-triangle duets. Not only Mrs Sculpin listened to the concert: the ghost of Marcus Magus, it seemed, had a craving for music, and he came drifting out of the centuries to hum, warble, whistle, tap in time, and applaud ecstatically at the end of each piece.

"Oh, good evening, Mr Magus," said Aunt Daisy, when he first made himself known. " I don't believe you have met my niece Nonnie."

"Delighted to heare you," (the ghost could not see them, of course, nor they, him, but Nonnie felt a cool puff of air on her right hand, as if invisible fingers had shaken it), "ah, Mozart, Mozart, whatte a genius! Ynne alle of time or space, backwardes or forwardes, I have never hearde another composer to touche hymme! And ytte is most interesting thatte you should have playede his musick tonighte, for, once or twyce lately, I have hearde Mozart's own voyce . . ."

"His voice?" said Nonnie, transfixed. *"You heard Mozart's voice?"*

"Yesse, child, of a surety. And inne a moste strange contexte."

"Context?" said John, who was not

familiar with this word. "What do you mean, context, Mr Magus?"

"Why, I hearde Herr Mozart conducting a parley withe two or three other folke who, to be sure, canne never have mette hym in true tyme or space - hee was talking with a Frenche commander yclept Napoleon, with Juliusse Caesar the Roman, with a lady hyght (I thynke) Jane Austen - they were alle, so farre as I could comprehende, immured together agaynst their wille, and greatly perplext as to how they mighte fynd the means to free themselves . . ."

"Mozart was shut up somewhere with *Jane Austen* and *Julius Caesar* and *Napoleon*? But how could that possibly be?"

"A most shockynge, evil enchantment, transgressing the boundaries of tyme. Some vile wytche must have done it! Pulling together four greate Personnes of fame and wisdome from the worlde's historie and confining them in one spotte agaynst their wille, of a surety for some evil purpose. It was a greate piece of wicked-nesse!"

"Oh well," said Mrs Sculpin, yawning, "I daresay it was just one of those TV quiz shows – *Lucky Lukie*, maybe, you know, the fellow who interviews people in the street for his programme. He met up with your sister Una not long ago. There's no end to the comical, clever things those fellows think up. Like *Desert Island Discs*, you know: they shut up Mozart and Napoleon and those other fellows on an island and make you guess which one will get away first. Now, dearies, time for bed! Nonnie wants to be off looking for her sister in the morning, and there's sure to be some nasty messages for John to wash off. Mr Mugus – if you're wakeful, why don't you go upstairs and have a nice chat with Colonel Njm?"

"Noe, noe, I thanke you, madam! Hee is of too high and grande a degree to discourse with soe humble a phantomme as myself."

"Oh, good gracious me, I don't think that's so at all," said Mrs. Sculpin, surprised. "I've always found him ever such a nice easy gentleman - not a bit stuck up or hard to please."

Yawning, she went upstairs.

"I do wonder *where* Mozart and those other people were shut up?" said Nonnie, as John made sure that Euston was safe in his basket by the kitchen stove.

"In the planet Sigma Nine, a smalle planet which lies under the power of a wicked enchantress, those four unfortunates are helde prisoner; ynne a specially constructed house yclept Pemberley," Marcus Magus informed her. "Mysse Austen, as I recalle, was greatly displeased, since shee was notte able to make progresse wyth a romantical tale she had begunne, in her owne daye, of two young personnes crost in love-"

"*Pride and Prejudice*, would that be? But-"

45

"And Napoleon was impatient to commence a greate battle – *Waterloo*, I thinke – and Mozart to worke on a masque or fantasy, *The Magic Flute* . . . Goodnyght, my young friends. Your musick has set my aged Vapours a–tingling . . ."

Marcus Magus floated away to the warm cranny behind the kitchen chimney-breast which was his favourite resting-spot.

Chapter Five

Next morning dawned miserably cold and dark. Freezing fog hung around the chimney-pots of Rumbury Town, like smoke from the jaws of an ice-dragon.

"Winter's nearly here," said Mrs Sculpin.

Colonel Njm went off early to his research at the Unwellcome Institute, shouting a last stern command to his cat through the guest room door in a voice that made the whole house tremble to its foundations.

Breakfast that day in the Sculpin family was disrupted by two unexpected happenings. One of these was that, when Mrs Sculpin sliced off the top of her boiled egg, a small snake popped out at her. She let off a shriek that blew off the petals of the geranium on the kitchen windowsill.

Both John and Nonnie were quite paralysed with surprise at the sight of the snake, and sat staring; but Euston the cat was perfectly equal to the emergency. A week's frustration over not being allowed to go into the guest room and tear strips off the Colonel's pet came boiling out, and while everyone else was wondering how to tackle the snake, Euston had shot up on to the breakfast table and bitten it clean in half.

"Well – *I* don't know, I'm sure!" whimpered Mrs Sculpin rather shakily, staring first at her broken egg cup and then at Euston who, now on the floor, was triumphantly shaking the tail half of the snake. "Eggs with snakes in them! I shall write to the Consumers' Association. And to the Co-Op. Oh deary me! If I pour myself a cup of tea, *what's* going to come out of the spout?"

Fortunately, no scorpions were discovered in the teapot, but Mrs Sculpin, who hated snakes, was really upset by the occurrence, and even the prospect of going to a sale of grandfather clocks in Vicars Green Town Hall did not greatly cheer her.

The second upsetting event was the sight of an advertisement in the Rumbury Gazette. John, scanning the Personal Notices in order to find out what it cost to place an advertisement, discovered one which said: UNA SMITH. Relatives who wish to see her alive again had better produce the Jewel Seed.

"Oh, my gracious *saints*!" exclaimed Mrs Sculpin when her attention was drawn to this. "*Now* what? My poor nerves will soon be in tatters. Una must have been kidnapped! By some of these nasty African gorillas or Arabian Knights, I suppose. Oh, whatever shall we do? The Jewel Seed? What is the Jewel Seed? I've never even heard of it."

Neither Nonnie nor John had heard of the Jewel Seed. Nor had Mrs Stokes next-door. And it was no use trying to consult Marcus Magus; he could never be contacted before about eight o'clock in the evening.

"But who could have kidnapped Una?" said Nonnie. "And why?" She was terribly upset. Nothing like this had ever happened in the Smith family before. And why should it? The Smiths were ordinary people. Unless - unless - it had something to do with Una's power of telling extraordinary stories. There was something *special* about Una . . .

"Do you think," suggested John, "that they - whoever *they* are - have taken her off - like those people Mr Magus was telling us about last night?"

"You mean Napoleon and Mozart? To some peculiar planet?"

"Sigma Nine," said John.

"But why should they want to take

Una?" said Nonnie forlornly. "She's my favourite sister. But she's not *important*. Or – or is she?"

"She never had a Jewel Seed?"

"Goodness me, no! What is a Jewel Seed, anyway?"

"I dunno."

As John had no Objectionable Inscriptions to erase that morning, he accompanied Nonnie back to Forge Hill, in search of possible clues to Una's whereabouts.

They walked slowly past the clothes shop called Mrs Wednesday's, staring at the forest of gaudy shirts and pants and skirts that hung inside on rows of racks. A big new sign said: SHIRTS WANTED! Our new Winter Shirt Swop. Bring your old shirt and exchange for two of ours!

"I suppose I could exchange that old white shirt of Una's," said Nonnie. "It's too big for me, and the sleeves are much too long. And I suppose Una doesn't want it, or she wouldn't have left it behind. But I wouldn't like to do it till I've asked her. Anyway I don't much care for theirs. And I don't like *them*."

Two skinny girls with hair in spikes stood at the front of the shop, under the stuffed witch, wagging their heads to the music and staring scornfully at the passers-by. They stared specially scornfully at Nonnie and John.

"Want a new shirt, sonny boy?" one of them said to him.

"No thanks. But do you know where the Kirlylox people went?" he asked.

"Emigrated. All went off to Trinidad-"

"All died of PVC virus-" they both said at the same time.

"Thanks for nothing," John said.

"Why don't you ask at the estate agents?" suggested a wizened little man who was selling newspapers off a rack just outside. And he nodded at a sign that said: This Property Let by Hard Knox Ltd, Estate

Agents, Crow Street, Forge Hill.

"Good idea," said John. "Come on, Nonnie."

Nonnie, who had wandered in among the clothes racks and burrowed her way to the back of the shop, rejoined John looking puzzled. "They've a couple of dressmakers' dummies at the back," she said, "all wound about with Indian silk saris. One of them gave me a queer feeling – it looked like Una . . ."

"I was thinking about the Jewel Seed in the night," said John, "wondering what it was. Did Una have any jewellery? Might she have had something – something valuable that she didn't *know* was valuable?"

"No, I'm sure not," said Nonnie. "She doesn't even *like* jewellery. She only wears wooden jewels. What *is* a Jewel Seed, any-way?"

"Maybe," said John hopefully, "if you sow it, up comes a tree covered with jewels?"

"*That* doesn't sound likely to me!"

They made their way to the office of the estate agents Hard Knox Ltd in the next street but two. Here they had another disappointment, for the office had closed down, its windows were coated all over with white paint, on which somebody had scribbled: FIMBULWINTER'S COMING.

"What's Fimbulwinter?" asked John.

"No idea," said Nonnie, staring behind her with a frown.

"Well, it's certainly getting cold enough for *any* kind of winter. What's up?"

"That ugly little dog. It seems to be following us."

The little dog was *very* ugly - small, bandy-legged, white with patches of dirty brown, a spotty face, a sharp nose, and bulging eyes.

"It looks exactly like a dog that used to live in the house next-door to Granny," Nonnie said. "We always thought the lady who owned it had trained it to shoplift. It used to pinch workmen's lunch-boxes-"

At that moment the little dog neatly whipped a packet of sausages from a bag perched on a pushchair's undercarriage.

"Let's get away from it!" said Nonnie. "Nasty little beast. Someone might think it was ours, the way it keeps following us."

They raced back to the tube station, but the dog scurried after them pertinaceously, never more than four or five metres behind.

At the station, however, they managed to foil it by nipping on to a train just before the doors closed.

As the train slid away, they saw the dog left behind on the platform, staring up at the indicator as if memorising the information shown there.

And then, on the grimy glass of the carriage windowpane, Nonnie saw three notes form themselves as if drawn by an invisible finger – three crotchets:

followed by the words: APPLES SAVE UNA.

"Look, John – *look*!" gasped Nonnie, but the notes and letters faded as fast as they had come; by the time John turned his head, they were gone.

Chapter Six

Soon after Nonnie and John had left the Sculpin house, a poor old lady, shabbily dressed, with a woollen shawl over her head, came limping along Pond Walk and rang the doorbell of Number Five. Mrs Sculpin had not yet gone off to her sale of grandfather clocks, so she opened the front door.

"I don't need any new kitchens *or* any double-glazing, thank you," she said at once, "and I've got plenty of dusters and silver-cloths and furniture polish," she was going on, when the old lady interrupted her.

"It's not dusters or windows, dear, I was going to ask if you have any old shirts you wouldn't mind giving away for a good cause. The Distressed Old Fairy Persons Home at Earlswood, I expect you've heard of it?"

"Old *shirts*?" said Mrs Sculpin, caught off balance. "Um - well - yes, there might be an old one of my son's - if you'll wait a moment I'll see."

Being cautious and prudent, since there had been so many burglaries lately, she left the front door on the chain as she went upstairs. Nevertheless, when she came down again with a terribly ragged and worn blue denim of John's, she was annoyed to see that the old lady's nasty little dog had somehow managed to squeeze through the crack and had scurried right through the house to the yard at the back, where the washing was hanging. Mrs Sculpin had been pegging out kitchen towels and had left the back door open when the front doorbell rang.

"Come out of there, you nasty little beast!" called Mrs Sculpin sharply. And she was about to go after the dog when it came out of its own accord, in utter and abject terror, ears and tail as low as they would go, and the whites of its eyes bulging as big as poached eggs. Mrs Sculpin pushed the dog crossly out into the street and offered John's shirt to the old lady, who took it without much gratitude.

"You've not got a white shirt? This one's - well - rather *blue.*"

"Only my niece's, and I don't think she'd want to part with that - she was talking about cutting off the sleeves so it would be more comfortable-"

"Cutting off the *sleeves?*" The old lady seemed startled to death at this news. But she went on quickly, "Such a funny thing to do, you know! I don't suppose you'd *have* those sleeves - if she really has cut them off?"

"If she did, she probably burned them in the boiler," Mrs Sculpin said shortly. She was anxious to get off to her sale. "Well, *good* day–"

But she paused a minute, before shutting the front door, to stare after the old girl limping away up the street with her ugly little dog and shopping trolley.

"Somewhere I feel I've seen that woman before ... Now, I do wonder what scared that nasty little brute so much, in the back yard? Can't have been Euston, for he's fast asleep on John's bed ..."

Rumbury Tube Station is one of the deepest in London, since at this point the Northern line has to burrow under Rumbury Rise, which soars higher above sea level than any other point for miles around. So, to descend to the level of the train platforms, you have to ride on three very long escalators, each one the height of a five-storey house. This was one of the reasons why John Sculpin preferred to travel by bicycle. The advertisements alongside the Rumbury moving stairs had not been changed since 1980 and John had grown very bored with the same old instructions to take out a mortgage at the Rumbury Savings Bank or buy a hamburger at the Bagel Burger Bar (which had closed down more than five years ago).

But as John and Nonnie travelled homewards, he noticed that the advertisements were different. Every single one, all the way up the three flights of moving stairs, carried the same message, one word in each square frame: SAVE - UNA - FIND - THE - JEWEL - SEED.

"When Una was still living at home and going to school," said John, "did she have a garden or grow plants?"

"Yes, she loved gardening, she used to grow a lot of herbs and sweet-scented things. But Mrs Wednesday's horrible little dog from next-door used to come through the hedge and scratch up her seeds . . . I wonder if that *was* the same dog? It did

63

look just like it."

As John and Nonnie walked out of Rumbury Tube Station, large flakes of snow were starting to flutter out of a very grey sky.

"Snow already!" said John.

Nonnie was looking at the billboard of the Rumbury Evening News, which said: More Monster Fatalities. Rumbury Canal Problem.

They hurried back to the house in Pond Walk, which was empty, because Mrs Sculpin had gone off to her sale.

"Let's have a mug of hot chocolate," said John, and took the lid off the kettle. A small snake popped its head out. John, with great presence of mind, dumped the snake in the rubbish disposal unit (which Mrs Sculpin had bought at a church sale) and pressed the switch.

Nonnie had not noticed this. She was sitting at the kitchen table worrying.

"How can we save Una, how can we

find her? And I've hardly any money, I ought to get a job, I ought to pay your Mum some rent. Maybe if I ask at all the hairdressers in Rumbury High Street I might get news of Una. And one of them might take me on as a trainee."

"That's not a bad plan," said John, pouring the boiling water on to hot chocolate powder. "Maybe we should put an advertisement in a hairdressing journal."

"Saying what?"

"Saying we haven't got the Jewel Seed, I suppose. Then they might let Una go."

"If only we had some idea who *they* were . . ."

Nonnie had fetched down her white shirt and now cut off the sleeves, doing the job with Una's pair of Tibetan scissors, which had serrated teeth, like pinking shears, and cut a zigzag line.

"That's neat!" said John.

"It ought to mean the cloth won't

unravel, so I shan't need to hem it," said Nonnie, poking the cut-off sleeve ends into the boiler, where they burned with a bright green flame. "It's funny, Granny said something about Mrs Wednesday and the shirt at the time when I left home, which I didn't quite take in; something about her being light-fingered; but I *know* the shirt belongs to Una. I remember her making it, for a school project, when she was in the sixth form; she grew the flax herself, soaked it, pounded it, spun it, wove it into linen cloth, and cut out the shirt, without a pattern. It took her the whole of three terms, she only just finished it before she left school. And after all that she left home without it. See, here's her initials, I.U.S. for Imogen Una Smith, embroidered on the collar . . ."

Nonnie put on the shirt, over the green sweater she was wearing.

The doorbell rang.

"I'll go," said Nonnie, for John was doing a complicated repair job on the cuckoo clock combined with toaster which his mother had just bought. There was something distinctly wrong with its functioning: the cuckoo kept appearing through the toast slot, while the clock would only strike thirteen, and by that time the toast had been thoroughly burnt.

Outside the front door stood a very elegant lady looking superciliously up and down Pond Walk. She wore a black riding-hat, a short slender black car-coat with yellow trim, and black-and-yellow striped culottes. She had stepped out of an electric wheelchair and leaned nonchalantly on a Malacca cane.

"My dear!" she said to Nonnie. "I *do* believe that you are wearing my grand-mother's shirt! May I ask a boon of you? May I ask for it back? It is *such* an heirloom - otherwise, naturally, I should not trouble you over such a trifle-"

"*Mrs Wednesday*!"

"Ah - you recognise me!" the lady

laughed musically. "That, of course, makes everything so much more comfortable. My love, when I was away on a lecture tour, I do believe that your darling grandmother – such a sweet, wayward old soul! – must have removed the shirt from where it hung on my clothesline. My *own* grandmother made it, you see – and when it is washed it has to hang out for thirty-nine days for a reason which I won't go into on the public street."

"I'm afraid you are quite mistaken," said Nonnie with great politeness. "And if it was on your clothesline I can't think how it got there, for my sister Una made it at school, and she embroidered her initials on the collar; see, here, I.U.S., so I know it's hers."

"My darling grandmother's initials – Indira Undine Saturday – but *why*, child, have you cut off the sleeves – how could you have done such a thing – what have you done with them?"

"Burned them in the boiler," said

Nonnie.

"*What*?" The lady turned the colour
of pistachio ice cream.

At this moment Colonel Njm arrived home unusually early. In general, he remained at the Unwellcome Institute until after dark.

At the sight of the Colonel Mrs. Wednesday behaved oddly; she uttered a faint shriek, sprang into her electric wheel-chair, and whirred away in it so fast that she almost seemed to vanish. Her little dog went whimpering and scuttering along the street, some way behind her.

Colonel Njm did not observe any of this. He seemed put out, frowning and pre-occupied; he hardly noticed when Nonnie politely held the door for him.

"Have you seen my cat?" he snapped.

"No," said Nonnie, puzzled. "I thought it was shut up in your room—"

"I forgot to administer its pill."

The white lump he held in his hand was about the size of a ping pong ball.

"Is that a yeast pill?" said Nonnie, interested. "I bet Euston would love one too. He's crazy about yeast, Aunt Daisy says."

"No, it is *not*. And he certainly may not have one."

The Colonel strode upstairs, calling, "Puss! Puss!" in a loud, threatening tone.

But no reply could be heard from his room.

Chapter Seven

That evening everyone was tired: Mrs Sculpin, because she had pushed a grandfather clock full of apples all the way from Vicars Green in her wheeled shopping trolley, John because he had erased Objectionable Inscriptions from five different tube stations, Nonnie because she had walked the length of Rumbury High Street and asked for news of her sister Una at seventeen hairdressers' shops. None of them could help her, and none of them offered her a job.

Mrs Sculpin, though tired, was triumphant because the clock she bought had been a great bargain, only five pounds fifty pence, and the apples had been offered her, practically free, from a sinking barge.

"We'll have fish-and-chips for supper and apples after," she announced. "John, you can go down to the Cheery Sole and get us all a nice portion of plaice. Buy some for the Colonel too, he's partial to fish-and-chips."

"Okay, Ma," said John.

Nonnie said she would go too, and help carry.

It was not quite dark when they started, so John said to save time they might as well go the quick way to Rumbury High Street, along the canal path.

The town was very quiet as they walked along the towpath; even the starlings had nothing to say; and the reflections in the middle of the canal hung clear and still and sharp as razor-cuts. Near the bank the water was beginning to freeze.

"People will start skating on the canal soon, I shouldn't wonder," said John. "And that ought to make it harder for the Bootlace Monster to grab anyone – if there really is a Bootlace Monster—"

A short cobbled alley, Fishermen's Way, led from the canal to Rumbury High Street. In the middle of the cobbled track stood a red telephone kiosk, glowing like a beacon through the foggy dusk.

As John and Nonnie passed the phone box, the phone inside started to ring.

"Someone got a wrong number," said John. But, as the phone continued to ring and ring, he said, "Oh well, I may as well tell them they've only got through to the phone box."

He pulled open the door and picked up the receiver.

"John? Cousin John?" said the voice. "Please, I must talk to Nonnie!"

"Is that – *Una?*" John gasped.

"Una? It's Una?" cried Nonnie, listening outside the box. "Oh, quick, quick – let me talk to her!"

She squeezed into the box with John and took the phone from him.

"Una? Is that truly you? Have you really been kidnapped? Where are you?"

"Listen, Nonnie," said her sister's voice. "They've got me shut up – and they say they will put me in a Black Hole for ever unless you hand over the Jewel Seed. And they will keep Julius Caesar and Mozart and Jane Austen shut up as well – so she can never write *Pride and Prejudice* and Caesar can never invade Britain. There's a kind of cupboard in time–"

"But who are *they*? And where are you? And, Una, why do they want *you*?"

"They are the Winter People. I am in Nifleheim – deep, deep down. Wrap me in white, wrap me in white . . . Find the apples . . . Apple seed and apple thorn . . . Without the Seed, no life can be born . . . All they want is the Seed . . ."

Now Una's voice faded away and was replaced by what sounded like hurricane force winds.

"Oh, Una!" wailed Nonnie. "Where

have you gone? What is the Jewel Seed? Where is it?"

But no other message came through, though they waited by the phone box for twenty minutes.

"Well, this is no use," said John sensibly at the end of that time. "And Ma will be worrying. She'll think we've been swallowed by the monster. And it's getting awfully cold. We'd better get home and ask Marcus Magus for his advice."

So they hurried on to The Cheery Sole, which was doing brisk business on such a dismal cold evening, and stood in line, and bought large, hot, savoury-scented parcels of plaice and chips.

Returning home, they were so absorbed in talking over the mysterious call from Una, arguing over whether it really *had* been Una, and if so how she could possibly have known the number of the phone box, how she could have known they would be outside it just at that moment, how she could have got hold of the money for the call, who the Winter People might be, and what was the name of the place where Una was imprisoned – Nonnie thought it was Niffle-hime and John thought Nivv-lime – that they clean forgot about the night-time dangers of the tow-path and went back by the same way they had come. By now it had become quite dark and very foggy. Occasional street lamps threw only a very faint light along the towpath. Something small quietly scurried along the path behind them.

Nonnie was saying, "John, I'm sure it's my turn now, you've carried the shopping bag quite far enough–" and John was saying, "That's O.K., Nonnie, I'll take it as far as Barrel Wharf–" when Nonnie let out a sharp cry.

"Help! John! Something's got hold of my arm. Ugh! Let go! *Help*!"

John was a few paces ahead of her on the path. He turned, and saw his cousin struggling and bent almost double, as if she were being pulled violently backward by both elbows.

Chapter Eight

Murder!" gasped John. "I'm coming, Nonnie, here—"

Hastily dumping the bag of fish-and-chips on the grassy bank, he sprang back to help Nonnie tackle whatever had grabbed her. He found that a number of tendrils, like striped, lumpy rubber bands, were wrapped tightly round her arms. As he dragged at these, trying to loosen and pull them off, more and more of them came reaching out of the darkness; they started twisting and twining round his arms as well. They were cold and stretchy and strong as steel cable. Both he and Nonnie were being dragged with deadly and almost irresistible force towards the cold dark waters of the canal.

"What in the world *are* they? Horrible tangly things–!" Nonnie gulped. "Like wires–"

One of them flicked across her face and fastened round her neck. "Ugh! Aargh! It's throttling me!"

"We need a knife - to cut through them–"

But, alas, John's beloved Swiss Navy Knife, with its ninety-nine blades and its corkscrew, had been left at home, among the innards of the cuckoo clock.

"Pl - ugh - och - ochit -" mumbled Nonnie, through the tendrils that were now masking her mouth.

Very intelligently, John concluded that she must mean *pocket*, and he pushed his right hand, which luckily was still free, into her left-hand jeans pocket, and there found a pair of scissors - they were the very thing that was needed. Dragging them out, he began to snip and snap and slash at the strong, rubbery strands that curled and twisted and dragged them towards the water.

"Let go! Loosen up! Take that! Blimey, there's hundreds of them! Where do they come from?"

By huge good luck the Tibetan scissors, with their solid notched blades, had a powerful and speedy effect on the twining, grabbing strands; besides slicing through them, the thick copper blades seemed to burn and shrivel the rubbery tentacles, which curled up and shrank like scorching wool at every snap of the cutting edges. Fairly soon, John was able to drag himself free, and then do the same for Nonnie; both of them stood trembling, gulping air, getting their breath back – for both had been half-strangled – and gazing in horror at the black waters of the canal, which heaved up and down as if, below them, something huge still floated unseen, waiting for another chance to pounce.

"Let's get away from here," said John

hoarsely.

"The fish-and-chips–"

But the parcel of fish-and-chips had gone, had been whipped away with silent speed while they were still battling off the attack.

"Can't be helped," said Nonnie. "There's eggs in the pantry, I'll make an omelette. Nothing's going to make me go back *that* way again. What in the world was it, John, do you think?"

"Some kind of octopus?" guessed John. "Or a huge jellyfish? There's a thing called a Portuguese Man o' War that has hundreds of poisonous tentacles–"

"I'm coming up all over in itchy bumps," said Nonnie. "Wherever those strings touched me."

"Yes, I am too. Let's go."

As they hurried away, they did not notice that in the foggy distance, there was a slight splash and a loud gulp; then a faint series of diminishing barks. The monster had claimed some other victim.

Weak and breathless though they were, John and Nonnie ran all the way home.

Mrs Sculpin let out a frantic wail when she saw them.

"My sainted thingummy! What ever have you two been up to?"

"It was the m-m-m-monster!" gulped Nonnie. "I'm afraid it got off with the fish-and-chips—"

"*You never came by the towpath?* You saw the monster?"

"And now we're all covered in blisters—"

"You pair of little castaways!" cried Mrs Sculpin. "You cotton-witted little sketches! How could you be so bacon-brained? Oh I could shake you – taking such a risk! And losing all our suppers! And never thinking of *me* and *my* feelings – suppose the monster had eat you all up?"

Luckily at this moment Colonel Njm came downstairs, expecting fish-and-chips.

He had to be told the story of their escape. He seemed very much concerned, asked a great many questions, and recommended apple-juice, which, applied to their blisters, did indeed reduce the pain and swelling.

"I'll put a nice pizza in the oven, Colonel," said Mrs Sculpin. "It'll be ready in ten minutes. We could have had us an omelette but – would you believe it! – every single egg we broke had a snake inside. I'm going to give that dairy a real piece of my mind."

"Snakes, Mrs Sculpin? In the eggs? Oh, dear me–" the Colonel seemed deeply upset at this news, almost as if he felt it was his fault.

"Never you mind, Colonel dear, our cat Euston killed the lot of them. A real terror on snakes, Euston is. John, as you are near the set, just switch on Channel Nine, will you? It's that TV programme I like – *Lucky Lukie*, the quiz game, the fellow who lines up people in the street–"

Lucky Lukie, who soon appeared on the screen, was an active, dynamic question-master, leaping about like a firecracker, poking fun at the two teams he had assembled in Lincoln's Inn Fields, teasing and abusing

86

them.

"Right, now, you lot, here's the first question, it's an easy one. And if you set of dullards don't know the answer, let's hope someone from the other side does – dickory dock, who's inside the clock? And, while you're thinking, one for the other team – who are the Winter People? Come on, don't look so pie-faced–"

Colonel Njm, with what sounded like a muttered oath, swung round to leave the room.

"Excuse me – I cannot endure television – such dreadful vulgarisation of life-and-death matters–"

He shut the door behind him with a slam, and this seemed to upset the TV. The screen flashed white, then turned a dull red, and no thumps or kicks or pressing of different buttons on the control panel would restore it to proper functioning.

"Oh well," sighed Mrs Sculpin, "I did get it out of a builder's skip. Never mind, the pizza's just about done. Shame, though; I always enjoy that Lucky Lukie. He's a real clever fellow – chats up people in the street, asks them questions, always has something sparky to say. He stopped Una, two or three weeks ago, asked her something – I forget – but she was a match for him. She was cool as could be. John, be a dear and take up Colonel Njm's tray."

While John was upstairs the cat Euston shot in through his cat-flap at top speed. He seemed unusually dishevelled and wild-eyed, with patches of fur missing.

"*Euston*? What's up with you? Oh, dear, Nonnie, I think you are right, there's some nasty creature comes into that yard at night," said Mrs Sculpin, as John came downstairs. "The lights keep flashing on even when Euston's indoors. John, tomorrow morning I think you'd better sprinkle a handful of that Pest Peril Pepper about the place . . ."

After they had eaten their pizza they

planned to finish with apples. But it proved impossible to open the grandfather clock which, at present, still reclined in Mrs Sculpin's shopping trolley in the front hall, till John had time to mend it.

"That's funny," said Mr Sculpin, greatly perplexed, when no wrenching would open the door in the front. "It wasn't locked at the sale hall. And when I stopped by the canal to buy apples off the barge, it opened as easy as easy and I put the apples inside. Nice green ones they were. Granny Smiths. There's no key to the clock. They never gave me one."

"Well it seems to be locked now, all right," said John, gently prising at the door with a screwdriver.

They tried all the spare keys in the house, but none of them fitted the lock.

"Oh, well, drat it," yawned Mrs Sculpin. "I'm tired. I'm off to bed. And so should you two, pretty soon, after all you've been up to. Monsters! The idea! We'll find a way to open the clock in the morning."

After Mrs Sculpin had gone off to bed, Nonnie and John played a few flute-and-triangle duets, which brought Marcus Magus floating out of the past to listen and applaud.

They told him all that had been happening to them, and he went into a long and contemplative silence.

"Are you still there?" asked Nonnie after a while.

"Yesse, childe; I do but reflecte. – You are the youngest of nyne children, isse thatte notte soe?"

"Yes it is."

"Your mother was likewise the youngest of nyne?"

"Yes."

"And your lost sister is the eldest? Describe her."

"Well," said Nonnie after some thought, "she has very fair hair – and she's fond of apples. And she used to tell me stories, *beautiful* ones."

"Her natal day?"

"March twentieth."

"Aha! The firste daye of springe. Didde shee ever tell you a historie of a shepherd choosing a lyttle blue flowre out of a caverne filled with preciousse jewells?"

"Why yes, she did," said Nonnie in surpise. "But what has that to do with—"

"Itte may bee thatte yr revered Gueste upstairs is the one to whome you should turn for advyce. For whatte can hee be doing here, so farre from his owne playce?"

"He's doing research at the Unwellcome Institute," John said.

"Your sister spake of apples in that crie for helpe? And of a white garmente?"

"Yes. At least she said, 'Wrap me in white'."

"I thinke you should weare or carrie your whyte shirte at all times, in case you meet her."

"I have it on now, over my sweater."

"And she sange a melodie? And you saw the notes of thisse melodie on the train window?"

"Yes. The tune went—"

"Waite, childe, waite! Trie singinge or playinge the melodie againste the locke of the clocke."

"The clock? What has that to do—"

"Nothinge is happeninge by chance at present," said Marcus Magus.

But when they went into the front hall to act on his advice, they were angry and disconcerted to find that the grandfather clock was no longer there.

"Well, I'm blest! Look at that!" said John indignantly. "The front door lock's been cut right out - like the core of an apple—"

"The thieves took Aunt Daisy's shopping trolley too," said Nonnie, putting her head out of the front door. "For you can see wheel tracks in the snow along the pavement. It's snowing quite hard - they

92

can't have been gone more than a few minutes. There's two sets of footprints. Quick! Let's go after them."

She grabbed a coat.

"Waite, waite, my headstronge younge friends!" called Marcus Magus anxiously. But John and Nonnie set off running along Pond Walk in pursuit of the wheel tracks.

"I'm just fed up!" panted John. "These Winter People – whoever they are – seem to be closing in on us. First Una, then our fish-and-chips, now Ma's clock – it's got to stop–"

"Lucky Lukie said something about a clock," gulped Nonnie. "And he talked to Una – Aunt Daisy said – perhaps that's what started the whole thing–"

At the end of the street they met a policeman.

"Oh, hello, P.C. Finch," panted John. "Did you see anyone pushing a trolley with a grandfather clock on it? They just pinched it from our house, Number Five–"

"Yes, I did see two characters in black – they went that way towards the graveyard – wait, stop a minute, young 'uns, don't you go off so fast–"

But heedless of his warning cry they raced on their way. P.C. Finch took a step after them, then thought better of it, and started back towards Number Five, talking on his mobile phone as he went.

"If they've gone to the cemetery," puffed John as they ran uphill, "that gives us quite an advantage."

"Why?"

"Because I'm the cemetery warden. It's my second-string job. The place is a bit of a spooky tangle, but I know all the paths and I carry the keys–"

Rumbury Cemetery, as they approached it in fog and snow, did indeed look like a ghost forest. The overgrown bushes and trees drooped under their load of snowflakes, or vanished upwards into dappled haze.

But the trolley tracks could still be seen, leading through the wrought-iron gates, which somebody had left open, and along a narrow path between high clumps of bamboo.

"Why in the world would they want to come here?" gasped Nonnie.

"Shh! I think they must have stopped! Slow! Tiptoe!"

Caution was hardly needed in the muffling snow. John and Nonnie stole forward and peered round a cypress tree into a clearing, where two paths met. To their great astonishment they found the shopping trolley and clock stationary in the middle of the track. But the thieves could be heard not far off in the bushes, thumping and clinking.

"What can they be doing? Digging up graves? That's what it sounds like."

"Never mind! Now's our chance – quick!"

They darted forward noiselessly. John

pointed left, and they steered the trolley along a narrow winding path between overgrown conifers. After rounding a couple of corners they came to a brick tower in a small clearing. The tower was slender in girth but quite high. Nonnie, peering up, saw that its top was veiled in driving snow and mist.

"We can go inside – I have the key," John explained, and produced it from a cord round his neck.

"Goodness, John! How – how very efficient of you," said Nonnie, much impressed.

"You see I keep tools in the tower for clipping and chopping. Now you go in front and pull, I'll push at the back. Hoist it over the step – that's good. We can lock ourselves in."

"But they are sure to follow our tracks here."

"There's a phone to call the Parks Department, in case I ever find somebody who's lost and starving," John said, switching on a light. "What's the matter?"

"John! There's *blood* trickling out of the clock!"

Chapter Nine

An emergency meeting of the Grand and Ancient College of Siberian Witches had been hastily summoned and, for lack of a more suitable location, was being held in the Rumbury Canal Tunnel, where the cut ran westwards for a mile under the high dome of Rumbury Rise, before it emerged to cross the flat plain of Sadlers Green.

The delegates were huddled together like nesting rooks along the brick paved towpath, peevish and mumbling, silently struggling for better places while pretending to be unaware that they were doing so.

"Are we all here yet?" hissed the Convener, in a whisper that carried easily from end to end of the mile-long tunnel.

A fidgeting and shuffling and rustling followed, as heads and horns were counted.

"Azriel - Goontas - Mrs Nightshade - Wizard Wullie - Limping Len - Blacklassie - Num - Nga - Ulgan - Erlik—"

Then the response.

"Not all here yet, Mistress. More are still to come. And the two brethren with the clock, though close at hand, are not yet present."

"The shirt?"

"Very near also, but not yet in our possession."

A dry snarl of impatient rage met this news.

"Useless - idle - impotent - *blockheads*! Let the laggards be summoned *urgently*. The time draws on—"

A strange, soft, rattling sound began to pour out from each end of the tunnel, audible to bats and cats and dogs, but not to normal humans.

Candidates and late-comers far away

across the Atlantic and the Sahara heard it,
and hastened their pace.

The doorbell at Number Five, Pond Walk rang loudly, twice. Mrs Sculpin, who was upstairs winding her hair on to curlers, heard it, and began to grumble.

"Who on earth can it be at this time of night? And why don't those children answer the door, haven't heard them come by, they must still be up, the light's on downstairs."

The bell pealed again, so Aunt Daisy went crossly down in her dressing-gown and headscarf.

She snatched open the door, without noticing that the lock was missing, just as the bell rang for a fourth time.

"All right, all *right*, I'm not deaf, I heard you, what is it?"

Two skinny girls in tight-fitting T-shirts and trousers stood outside. Their faces were pale, their eyes glittered, their hair stood up in spikes.

They spoke together. "Oh, hi, Mrs S, we're collecting ashes for a folk sculpture exhibition to be held on Rumbury Waste next summer – would you be able to let us have a couple of buckets of household ash?"

"*Ash*? You come here at this hour of night asking for *ash*? And how in the world is sculpture going to be made out of ash, may I ask?"

"Ashes make brilliant material for sculpture, Mrs S, just brilliant, you bind them together with epoxy resin. Now if we could just have a pailful or two from your boiler (I expect you empty out the ashes every night?) – just tell us where your back yard is, or where you throw out the ashes, we have shovels and buckets, you won't be put to the least trouble—?"

"Well, *I* dunno," said Mrs Sculpin, "I never heard anything of the sort before in all my born days, collecting ashes in the middle of the night; still, please yourselves, the yard's out through the kitchen door, the ash heap's down at the far end, take as much as you fancy. There's lights that'll come on as you go outside. But hurry up! And mind, when you come back in, that you don't track any ashy footprints over my kitchen floor."

The girls made haste to follow her directions, scurrying out of the back door, whispering together as they went.

Mrs Sculpin sat down, resignedly, at the kitchen table, to wait for their return. Instead, after a couple of minutes, a terrific hubbub broke out in the back yard. There were shrieks, gasps, wails, thumps, and a very unusual snuffling sound.

Then a long, long silence.

Mrs Sculpin put her head out of the back door. But there was nothing to be seen. Only the radiance from the sensor lights, shining on ash-sprinkled snow.

"Well, I dunno," said Mrs Sculpin for the second time. "I'm certainly not going out there. No way. Can those girls have done a bunk over the garden wall? And where can John and Nonnie have got to?

It's long past their bedtime."

She went back into the front hall and noticed, now, that the clock was missing.

"Well I never! Where's my clock? And my trolley? What's going *on* round here?"

The doorbell rang again.

The tower in the middle of Rumbury Cemetery was called Lady Ermintruda's Tower, because it had been built in memory of that lady by her sorrowing father. No one could remember exactly what her history had been, but no doubt it was very sad.

Inside this tower John and Nonnie faced one another, trembling, over the grandfather clock.

"We've got to get it open, right away."

"You don't think we should wheel it home first?"

"But we have to see what's in it. And those people are probably outside."

"Well – that's true."

"Marcus Magus said play the tune against the lock – those three notes that Una sang – that I saw written on the train window–"

Like John, Nonnie wore a cord around her neck. On hers was slung the little bone pipe that her parents had sent her from the Himalayas. Now she unslung this pipe and played three soft notes on it, kneeling by the clock, holding the pipe very close to the keyhole.

Nothing happened.

"Maybe we should sing?" suggested John. "After the pipe music?"

"Sing what?"

"You sing 'Wrap her in white'. I'll sing 'Apples, apples'."

They did so. Several minutes passed with no result. But then, slowly, gently, the lock clicked, the hinges creaked, the door on the clock fractionally shifted. Trembling with cold and terror and suspense, Nonnie lifted the door, very slowly and gingerly, exposing to view a pair of thin hands, crossed one over the other, and tightly bound together round the wrists by a thick skein of pale-gold hair.

"I don't believe it!" whispered Nonnie in horror. "Those are *Una's* hands! That's her walnut-wood ring. I'd recognise it anywhere. But where is the rest of her?"

"She's been stuck inside the clock, I suppose."

Very carefully, John touched the hands, and said, "They are warm. I can feel a pulse, just. She's alive. But whoever squeezed her in there? And how in the world are we ever going to get her out?"

"We'll have to break the clock."

"But how could we do that without harming her? And she's hurt already. That blood—"

The telephone rang, making them both jump. John picked up the receiver.

"Hullo?" he said nervously.

A loud, rasping voice in his ear hissed,

"This is the Queen of Winter! You must give us back the clock, it is ours. And the shirt! Or your lives will be worth no more than a dead leaf. Give us the Jewel Seed!"

John answered politely, "We can't give them to you. The clock belongs to us. My mother bought it. And the shirt belongs to my cousin. And we don't *have* the Jewel Seed. We don't even know what it is."

He replaced the receiver. The phone instantly began to ring again. "Oh, bother!" said John.

"Don't answer it," said Nonnie.

But John had already picked up the receiver.

This time it was the voice of Marcus Magus.

"That was well answered, lad! Nowe, singe the rune agayne – continue singing to loosen the lock of the clocke – singe, singe! . . ."

So they knelt by the clock chanting 'Apples, apples,' and 'Wrap her in white,' while slowly, splinter by splinter, shard by shard, the clock crumbled apart until it had completely collapsed into a pile of shavings and sawdust on the stone floor. Curled limply among the heap of shavings, pale and bloodstained, wrapped in moss, tied at the wrists and ankles by her own hair, lay Nonnie's eldest sister. By her head stood a small basket of green crystal apples.

"It's Una! It *is* Una! But – oh, John – she's bald! Someone shaved off all her hair. Oh, poor Una! John, is she alive?"

"Yes, she's breathing," said John steadily. "And I don't believe she's even very badly hurt – the blood seems to come mostly from cuts and scrapes where they crammed her into the clock."

"We must get her to a hospital. Can we call the emergency services?"

"No, only the Parks Department from here."

John tried the Parks Department number. But all he got was a recorded message telling him that due to shortage of staff the office would not be open until nine a.m., and to call again then.

"What'll we do?" said Nonnie.

"I'll switch the light on in the top room. The police will be sure to see that, and they'll come. Mr Finch must have reported our burglar by now."

He ran up the circular stairs. Nonnie, meanwhile, with her copper scissors, sliced through the strands of hair that tied Una's wrists, and gently rubbed her ice-cold hands and cheeks. She took off the voluminous white linen shirt, wrapped it round her sister, and put Una's arms through the sleeve holes.

"Una!" she whispered. "Can you hear me?"

No reply.

John came running down the stairs, big-eyed.

"I saw an awfully queer thing from the window. The path that leads to the canal – I saw a whole procession of people walking along it. They were dressed in black. And – this is the craziest thing of all – they were all balancing tombstones on their heads. Do you suppose that was what we heard in the bushes? Them digging up the tombstones? They look like professors in huge mortarboards. Where can they be going?"

"Goodness knows! I hope the police come soon," said Nonnie, shivering. Then she looked past John and let out a gasp.

"Colonel Njm!"

John whirled round.

The upstairs room of the tower had undoubtedly been empty when he went up to switch on the light. But now here, walking down the stairs, came Colonel Njm in his long dark overcoat and slanting, broad-brimmed hat. He moved very slowly, and appeared to grow in size at each step. In his hand he held a long staff. On his shoulders perched two huge black birds. A freezing draught accompanied him. The air all around him seemed to burn with a dark glow.

Two loud raps sounded on the door of the tower.

"Who's there?" called Nonnie nervously. "Is that the police?"

"No. It is the Winter People!"

Chapter Ten

"Oh, good evening, P.C. Finch," said Mrs Sculpin, all in a puzzle, to the policeman who stood on her front doorstep. "How can I help you? Mind you, there *have* been some very funny goings-on round here."

"I understand that you had a break-in? And that your clock was stolen?" said P.C. Finch.

"We did? Who told you that? Well, it's true, I did ask myself where the clock had gone." Now, for the first time, Mrs Sculpin noticed the hole cut in her front door and let out an indignant cry. "My sakes! Just look at that hole in the door! Somebody pinched the lock! What next, I'd like to know? And there's something *very* peculiar going on in our back yard, a pretty kettle of fish, if you ask me—"

"In your yard, Mrs Sculpin?"

"Yes, two young girls went out there looking for ashes, and they never came back."

"Shall I just take a look?"

P.C. Finch stepped out into the back yard, where the sensor lights still shone, as if some person or persons were already there.

Almost at once, Mrs Sculpin heard a scuffle and a shout. And, immediately after, the policeman whisked in again at top speed, looking highly discomposed, with his canister of repellent gas uncapped.

"You're quite right, Mrs Sculpin. There's something there that shouldn't be there, at the far end," he said. "It took a swipe at me, so I gave it a squirt of gas. But I think it would be best to wait for daylight on that one, Mrs Sculpin, if it's all the same to you. I would not go out there, just at present. And I would advise the rest of your household to follow the same advice."

"But what about those two girls? And my son John and my niece Nonnie?" wailed Mrs Sculpin.

"I dunno about the girls. But your son John and your niece Nonnie were last seen in Pond Walk proceeding in the direction of the graveyard, in pursuit of the malefactors who absconded with your clock," P.C. Finch told her. "A squad car has been summoned to go to their aid. I will now proceed to contact Rumbury Central."

He did so, on his mobile phone, and listened with an expression of growing astonishment.

In Lady Ermintruda's Tower John and Nonnie watched, petrified, as Colonel Njm pointed one, slightly luminous, finger at the door.

Despite being locked, it slowly opened, to reveal Mrs Wednesday standing on the threshold.

When she saw the Colonel she let out a faint moan, as if she were suffering from heartburn, and looked as if she would have liked to back away, but lacked the strength to do so.

The Colonel began to speak, in slow, biting words.

"*Wretch!* Not only are you a traitor to me, but to your own evil faction as well. While they assemble and argue, you plan to make off with the treasure. Do not deny. It is so! But you have failed, in spite of all your cunning. You have lost the Jewel Seed."

"Aaaaaah!" she wailed.

"You had it under your hand, in Sesame Green, but now it is lost to you for ever. Iduun has been wrapped in her mantle of white. At last! She will be restored to her full power. As for you - scum of the universe! - I cannot destroy you entirely, but I can reduce you to your components."

"Aaaaah – lord! No!" quavered Mrs Wednesday, but already she was shrinking and crumbling, as the clock had done, and soon she was reduced to a handful of black dust like volcanic lava that lay on the snowy path.

"Now," said Colonel Njm, turning to Nonnie and John, "human hands are needed for this part of the rite. But you will be protected, fear not. Lift Iduun gently. Place her on the trolley. Convey her back to your living-place. She will not be fully recovered until sunrise, until you have given her full, faithful assistance."

Greatly puzzled, but trusting the Colonel's authority, they hoisted Una as best they could on to Mrs Sculpin's shopping trolley. Nonnie carried the basket of apples. They shone, faintly, like mother-of-pearl.

"Now, home – with all speed," said the Colonel. "Pay no heed to anything you may hear."

What they did hear was quite terrifying. Great shadowy figures seemed to be all about the cemetery, looming high above the trees. As they pushed the stretcher along the narrow snowy paths, among the dark thickset bushes, loud noises exploded all around them. Yells and screeches and howls of utter dismay and despair and agony echoed from the direction of the canal. It sounded as if a whole multitude of creatures, not all human, were suffering some unbelievably grisly fate.

"What do you think is *happening*?" croaked John, and Nonnie, trembling, said, "Let's hurry – let's get away as quick as we can."

"Pay no heed," said the Colonel, who accompanied them, limping slightly, while his two large black birds flew overhead. "Pay no heed. It is merely my servant, Iormungandr, despatching my enemies."

At Number Five, Pond Walk, they found Mrs Sculpin in a high state of anxiety, with a kettle full of boiling water and several plates of sandwiches cut.

When she saw Una, pallid, bruised, shaved, and lying unconscious on the stretcher, Aunt Daisy let out a long lamenting wail.

"Oh, that poor darling girl, my poor dear Una, what have they ever *done* to her? Oh, just look at her hands, all bruised, and her poor feet, all cut – where *was* she? And her beautiful hair all shaved off as if she was one of those co-operators – the monsters! Where did you find her?"

"She was in the clock," said Colonel Njm. "And before that, in outer space, in the planet Sigma Nine. But now, soon, she will be well again and returned to her proper place. See, already her hair commences to grow."

He was right, it did: a faint frosty shine had begun to prickle over her bare scalp.

"When we have disposed of the Jewel

Seed, it will grow even faster," said the Colonel.

"The Jewel Seed?"

"Somewhere in this house it lies hidden at present," said the Colonel. "It had been sewn into the sleeve of the white shirt. So much we knew, but not where the shirt itself would next be found. For it is continually destroyed and re-fashioned, like the leaves of trees, and so must be, from age to age, for ever."

"But the shirt-sleeves were all burned up?"

"Then the seed must lie among the ashes. The seed is indestructible."

"Oh - I know!" exclaimed Aunt Daisy, suddenly enlightened. "A tiny, tiny red stone, Colonel?"

He nodded.

"I found it when I riddled out the boiler ashes before supper. I put it in one of Nonnie's little boxes - fetch it, Nonnie, do, there's a dear. It's upstairs on your shelf."

Nonnie found and brought down a tiny enamel box, one of her collection, which now contained a red stone in it about the size of a tomato seed.

"That little object has generated a lot of harm," said the Colonel. "The tricker, Loki, cast it into a field of flax to cause strife and dissension among gods and men. He loves to do such mischief. But now it shall cause no more trouble. I shall blow it away into the deepest recesses of Ginnunga-gap, where none may find it for many eternities."

He stepped towards the back door.

"Oh, I wouldn't go out there, Colonel dear! Not just now! Not till P.C. Finch has been again and disinfected the yard," Mrs Sculpin hastily informed him. "There's something really nasty out there: in fact I think it might be the Bootlace Monster, come up out of the water."

"Do not disturb yourself, my friend. The beast out there is merely my bond-servant, my cat, Iormungandr," Colonel Njm told her, and he stepped out of the back door and could be heard addressing some very severe words of command to whatever was outside. An explosion of loud hissing responded to his order.

"Now the Jewel Seed is well on its way to uttermost distances and can do no further mischief," the Colonel announced, after a short time, coming back into the kitchen and absently helping himself to a cucumber sandwich.

"But what about the thing out in the yard?" said Mrs Sculpin.

"That I regret. It is the Midgard Serpent, Iormungandr, my bond-beast, who, by my ordinance, lies coiled three times round the circuit of the globe. But, at need, he accompanies me in the guise of a cat. Only," acknowledged Colonel Njm, "I was obliged to administer to him a daily pill, to keep him within his cat-shape, and when, at times, I omitted to do this, he would rampage forth in his own shape to lurk in the canal and prey upon passers by. It was unfortunate. I am sorry for that."

"Oh, I see," said Mrs Sculpin rather faintly. "I suppose it was Eeyore-whatever-you-said who kept dropping those snakes about the house?"

"I must beg your forgiveness for that also," apologised the Colonel. "I guarantee that it shall occur no more. No indeed; now that our beloved Iduun is returned to us, we shall travel back to our own place."

"Iduun?"

"There she lies, soon to be restored to health – Iduun, daughter of the gods, the Queen of Spring. Sing to her, my friends – that will hasten her recovery."

"What should we sing?" asked Nonnie.

"Summer is icumen in," suggested Marcus Magus, who had been taking a keen, if unseen, interest in all these revelations.

So John and Nonnie sang:

"Summer is icumen in,
    Loude sing cuckoo!
Bloweth seed and groweth mead
Now springs the wood anew . . ."

They sang it round and round, for it is a song without beginning or end, and, after the ninth repetition, the cuckoo in the mended toaster suddenly put its head out of the proper hole and shouted "Cuckoo!" and Una stretched her arms and yawned, and smiled, sat up, and said, "Good heavens! I must have been asleep for a long time. How did I get here?"

"A long time indeed," agreed Colonel Njm gravely. "Since the autumn leaves fell from the branches. And you would have slept until the pages of time were all turned had not this pair come to your aid."

"Oh, Una! Are you truly all right? What happened to you?" Nonnie cried, giving her sister a warm hug.

"It was after that television fellow met me in the street," remembered Una. "Lucky Loki, was that his name? He asked some question about lucky charms. And I told him about finding a little red stone in the seed-pocket of an apple-core - I thought it must be lucky - so I kept it and sewed it into the cuff of my shirt-sleeve - I thought it might be a talisman. But then I kept seeing an old lady who looked like Mrs Wednesday - and her horrible little dog. What happened to her dog, by the way?"

"My bond-servant ate it," said Colonel Njm.

"Oh! And two girls with spiky hair kept following me about . . . I'm not sure what happened after that. But then I found myself shut up somewhere terribly cold and dark, in outer space, down below the bottom of everything . . . and I was told that unless I gave them the Jewel Seed a lot of things would never happen . . . spring would never come again, and America would never be discovered, and Jane Austen would never write *Pride and Prejudice* and Shakespeare would never write *Hamlet*, and people would start dying at the age of three . . . there would be a fold in time that nobody could get past. So I told them I didn't know where the shirt was."

"Iduun must re-fashion her shirt every new season," said Colonel Njm, nodding gravely. "And the old one vanishes into the limbo of time."

"So," went on Una, "I told them the shirt might be at Granny's house, unless she had given it to a jumble sale. Then, I think, they shut me in the clock – something to do with beginning the fold in time . . ."

As she told this story, Una's hair had grown another inch. Now it was down to her shoulders.

"Dearie, wouldn't you like a nice cup of tea?" said her Aunt Daisy.

"What I'd really like is one of those apples."

Una reached out a thin white arm and took one of the green glowing crystal apples from the basket.

"But–" began Nonnie. To her petrified astonishment, her sister bit into the apple as if it were a fresh fruit. And, as she did so, it became a fresh fruit.

Colonel Njm smiled for the first time.

"Those are the apples that renew eternal life in the gods," he said. "Now we know that Iduun will soon be better."

Nonnie said anxiously, "But you are *Una*, aren't you? My big sister Una? Who used to help me with my schoolwork? And – and tell me stories?" Her voice quivered a little.

"I was your sister for a term of life," Una said, taking her hand. "I remember it all now. The fold has unfolded. You are part of me and I shall always remember happy days at Sesame Green."

"But – but now? Won't you come back? And be our Una again?"

"Every springtime I shall come back," Una began, but Colonel Njm said, "The tasks of the immortals, child, are greater than your humble human affairs. You should be proud that you have been permitted to help the Lady Iduun escape her captors and return to her true sphere. Each year she will reward you with returning spring."

A long silence followed. Everybody seemed a little dazed with this idea.

Then John asked suddenly, "Who was that old girl, Mrs Wednesday? Why did she keep bobbing up? Why did she want Una's shirt?"

The Colonel's face darkened. A chill wind seemed to sweep through the room.

"She was once my wife," Colonel Njm growled. "But – we parted. She is a tool of darkness and a traitor to light. I am glad to think that she has now lost her power for many eternities."

"Who are the Winter People?"

"They are our enemies," said the Colonel hastily. "We will think no more of them. Accursed race. Their wish is to bring about the Fimbulwinter – the endless winter without hope of spring which would result in the downfall of the immortal gods. But – the Midgard Serpent has routed them for now."

"Will it ever–?"

"We will think no more of them," repeated the Colonel sternly. "Now, my lady, it is time for us to be gone. The Wanderer must depart on his endless road."

He extended a hand, and Una took it. As she stood up, her long, flax-coloured hair fell in a shining cascade to her ankles. She wore a white shift of smooth, creaseless material that glistened faintly. She kissed John and Nonnie and, smiling, said, "Give my love to Duessa, Tess, Quad, Quintus, Sexty, Seppy and Tavy."

The Colonel, bowing, said, "I thank you, Mrs Sculpin, for your hospitality."

"Oh, Colonel! I'm sure you were a model lodger! And you are welcome again *any* time. Any time! But, as for your Midgard Pusscat, no! There I do draw the line!"

The Colonel led Una to the door, where they were seen to shine briefly and then evaporate like steam from a kettle. Outside the kitchen window could be seen the first gleam of the rising sun. Three tremendously loud musical notes, like the sound of a gong, echoed momentarily over the roofs of Rumbury Town, then faded away into the distance and were gone.

"We shall see them noe more," said Marcus Magus.

"Oh, dear!" said Mrs Sculpin faintly. "I'm sure it's all too much for me. Dear little Una going off like that. The Goddess of Spring! What next, I'd like to know? And that Colonel Njm – who was he, then?"

"The Wanderer," Marcus Magus told her.

"Who's he, when he's at home?"

"He's *never* at home. He is the leader of the Old Gods, forever following his stern line of dutie."

"Well, whatever next? I'm off to bed," said Aunt Daisy, tired at the very thought, and went slowly upstairs. "You two had better get some shut-eye too," she called back.

Nonnie could not speak. Her throat was seized up, too tight for tears. The realisation that your beloved elder sister has all along been the Goddess of Spring is not something that can be taken in all at once.

"Listen!" said Marcus Magus. "I can heare voices. Listen!"

They waited, stock-still, holding their breath, listening. And heard what sounded like a tea party in progress: the clink of cups and saucers, pleasant voices, friendly laughter, silver spoons tinkling against china.

"Another slice of cake, dear Herr Mozart? More tea?"

"No, I thank you, Fraulein Austen."

"Well, General, this has been so very pleasant "

"I am indeed happy, my dear sir, to have made your acquaintance."

"I fear it may be some long time before we have the chance to meet again."

"Back, now, to our unfinished labours."

"I wish you good fortune in the battle, my dear confrere—"

"And to you, a safe crossing—"

"Auf wiedersehen, Fraulein Austen!"

"I shall think of you, dear Herr Mozart, every time that I sit down to the pianoforte."

"Crumbs!" said John Sculpin, yawning. "What a queer time of day to choose for a tea party. Must be in some other time zone."

As Nonnie, dead tired, sank to sleep in her bed, she thought she heard her sister Una's voice: "*Once upon a time there was a poor shepherd. And he found an opening leading into a mountain glacier, and ventured inside, into a great cave, whose walls gleamed with precious stones. And a lady greeted him, who held in her hand a little bunch of blue flowers . . .*"

Next day Nonnie found herself a trainee job in a new hairdressing establishment, Miss Tresses, which had just opened in

Rumbury High Street.

And Rumbury Council cleaning trucks had a most difficult time carting away and disposing of four hundred tonnes of black shoelaces found along the towpath of the Rumbury Canal.

FOG HOUNDS, WIND CAT, SEA MICE
Joan Aiken

Three spellbinding stories in one book, from a magical storyteller.

The Fog Hounds are mysterious – and deadly. They roam the land from dusk to dawn. No-one who is chased by them ever lives to tell the tale. But Tad is not afraid. Tad wants one for himself. And when he comes face to face with a Fog Hound puppy, things can never be the same again . . .

The Wind Cat and the Sea Mice have equally strange tales to tell . . .

Another fantasy story from Hodder Children's Books

THE DRAGON CHARMER
Douglas Hill

A dragon's scream as chilling and eerie as the howl of mountain winds.

Elynne longs to be a dragon charmer like her father, but the ferocious creatures terrify her. Then the annual migration brings a rare royal dragon. A Crimson Queen.

Soon the Queen gives birth to a baby. A dragon prince at once in mortal danger. Will Elynne – timid, mouse-like Elynne – find the courage to protect him?

ORDER FORM

0 340 68741 X   *THE DRAGON CHARMER*   £3.99
              Douglas Hill

0 340 68131 4   *FOG HOUNDS, WIND CAT, SEA MICE*   £
              Joan Aiken

----

*All Hodder Children's books are available at your local bookshop or newsagent,
or can be ordered direct from the publisher. Just tick the titles you want and fill
in the form below. Prices and availability subject to change without notice.*

Hodder Children's Books, Cash Sales Department, Bookpoint, 39
Milton Park, Abingdon, OXON, OX14 4TD, UK. If you have a credit
card you may order by telephone – (01235) 831700.

Please enclose a cheque or postal order made payable to Bookpoint
Ltd to the value of the cover price and allow the following for postage
and packing: UK & BFPO – £1.00 for the first book, 50p for the
second book, and 30p for each additional book ordered up to a
maximum charge of £3.00.
OVERSEAS & EIRE – £2.00 for the first book, £1.00 for the second
book, and 50p for each additional book.

Name
....
Address.
....
....
....

If you would prefer to pay by credit card, please complete:

Please debit my Visa/ Access/ Diner's Club/ American Express
(delete as applicable) card no:

Signature
....

Expiry Date
....